PUFFIN BOOKS

SUPER MOLLY AND THE LOLLY RESCUE

Daniel Postgate lives in Whitstable, Kent. He has worked as a newspaper cartoonist for many years and more recently has written and illustrated a number of children's books. He likes swimming, walking, cooking and watching the telly.

Daniel Postgate

Super Molly and the Lolly Rescue

PUFFIN BOOKS

Wicklow County Council
County Library Services

PUFFIN BOOKS

Published by the Penguin Group
Penguin Books Ltd, 27 Wrights Lane, London W8 5TZ, England
Penguin Putnam Inc., 375 Hudson Street, New York, New York 10014, USA
Penguin Books Australia Ltd, Ringwood, Victoria, Australia
Penguin Books Canada Ltd, 10 Alcorn Avenue, Toronto, Ontario, Canada M4V 3B2
Penguin Books (NZ) Ltd, 182–190 Wairau Road, Auckland 10, New Zealand

Penguin Books Ltd, Registered Offices: Harmondsworth, Middlesex, England

First published 1998
3 5 7 9 10 8 6 4 2

Copyright © Daniel Postgate, 1998
All rights reserved

The moral right of the author/illustrator has been asserted

Filmset in Times New Roman

Printed in Hong Kong by Midas Printing Ltd

Except in the United States of America, this book is sold subject to the condition that
it shall not, by way of trade or otherwise, be lent, re-sold, hired out, or otherwise
circulated without the publisher's prior consent in any form of binding or cover
other than that in which it is published and without a similar condition including
this condition being imposed on the subsequent purchaser

British Library Cataloguing in Publication Data
A CIP catalogue record for this book is available from the British Library

ISBN 0–140–38228–3

WICKLOW COUNTY COUNCIL

Date Recd...... 2/05/00

Inv. No. 2596

Acc. No. ...... 102923)

Class No. ...... JF

Price ...... £3·99

For Oliver

Contents

1. Missing

Molly was an ordinary sort of girl in every way, until one day she had an extraordinary adventure, and afterwards she was never the same again. This is what happened.

One morning, Molly woke up to a very quiet house. Normally it was full of the sound of doors banging,

the toilet flushing, and Mum
shouting, "Get up, Molly – time for
school!" But this morning –
nothing. And when Molly got up
and went downstairs, there was
absolutely no one there, except Mr
Fluffy, the cat, asleep in the
kitchen. She searched all around the

house but it was as if her parents had simply *disappeared*. It was all very scary indeed. Bewildered, Molly sat down at the kitchen table. That was when she found the note, stuffed between the marmalade and the cornflakes. This is what it said:

We have stolen your parents.
Find them if you can!
Love from the WWI.

"The WWI? Who are they?" Molly wondered. She poured herself a bowl of cereal and munched on it thoughtfully. It all seemed so peculiar that Molly decided she must still be asleep and dreaming. Perhaps if she shouted very, very loud she would wake herself up. She tried it, but all that happened was that Mr Fluffy shot across the kitchen floor and out through the cat flap. So then she realized she *wasn't* asleep and her parents *had* been stolen by the WWI (whoever they were). The best thing she could do was to go and see Grandad.

"Maybe he'll know who the WWI are," she thought. "After all, he does know just about everything about everything." So that's what she did.

2. Revelation

Grandad was outside his garden shed keeping an eye on his prize cucumbers. He was very good at growing cucumbers and had won more trophies for them than he could fit on his mantelpiece to prove it.

"Hello, young Molly!" he said. "Why aren't you at school?"

"Because I find myself in a very

extraordinary situation, Grandad,"
she told him.

"Oh yes?" he said. "You tell
your old Grandad all about it."
Then he settled down on his garden
chair and closed his eyes.

"Have you ever heard of the
WWI?" she asked.

Molly had never seen the old
chap move so fast. He leapt a good

two metres in the air and landed flat
on his feet. "What have they done?"
he asked in a hoarse whisper.

"They've stolen Mum and Dad,"
Molly said, and handed him the
note she had found.

Grandad fell back into his chair.
When he looked at Molly, his eyes
seemed tired and sad.

"My dear child," he said, "I have no choice but to tell you something which you were never supposed to know. You must swear to keep it a secret."

"I swear!" swore Molly.

Grandad poured himself a cup of

tea from his flask, took a sip and then told her an amazing story.

"In this town of Plumston, many years ago, there lived a young woman. She was ever so nice and spent a great deal of her time repairing furniture for the local charity shop. Furniture was her life and she dreamed of opening a shop of her own. Then one day, she discovered she had superhuman powers. But, instead of becoming a superhero and putting her powers to good use, she decided to become a witch and be bad. She embarked on a career of such naughtiness that – well, frankly, words fail me. Not satisfied with being bad on her own, she put some local women under a dreadful spell and formed the Wicked Women's Institute."

"The WWI!" Molly cried.

"That's right!" said Grandad. "Her band of wicked women sold home-made pies and cakes which caused illness throughout the district. They took the elderly out on day trips to the seaside and *left them there*. You couldn't even walk the streets of Plumston without being terrorized by gangs of wicked women demanding money for charities that didn't even *exist*."

"How terrible!" said Molly. "So what happened?"

"Well," said Grandad, "it turned out that superhuman powers ran in the rest of the young woman's family.

She had a brother and sister who found they were superhuman too, but they chose to be good. They drove their wicked sister, the Scarlet Sorceress as she liked to be known, out of Plumston for ever. She has never returned . . . UNTIL NOW."

Grandad leaned forward, and almost in a whisper said, "I was that brother, your Great Aunt Nelly was that sister, and the Scarlet Sorceress was your long-lost Great Aunt Gerty."

"WOW!" Molly cried. "But why haven't you told me this before?"

"Because your mother never wanted you to know," said Grandad. "She thinks this superhero business is all a bit . . . silly."

"Well, silly or not, I know about it now," Molly said. "So what's next?"

"That's the spirit, old girl!" cried Grandad. "First I must change into my superhero disguise and become ...." There was a puff of smoke and when it cleared . . .

there stood Grandad all dressed in green. "CAPTAIN CUCUMBER!"

3. Snuffles

Captain Cucumber finished off his tea in one mighty gulp.

"Right," he said. "Now we must find those parents of yours. Where's Snuffles . . . SNUFFLES?!"

Grandad's trusty old dog, Snuffles, trotted cheerfully out from behind the hedge, but when he saw his master dressed in the strange, green costume, he froze.

"Yes, old chap," said the Captain. "Duty calls once more."

In a flurry of fur and fleas, Snuffles spun round and round, and when he stopped, he was wearing a little brown mask and cape.

"As you see, sweetheart, Snuffles has superpowers too," said the

Captain. "Meet Super Snuffles!"

"Fair enough," said Molly.

The Captain held out the note from the WWI for Super Snuffles to sniff. At once, the mangy old hound started howling and scratching the earth.

"He's ready to go!" cried the Captain. "Quick, Molly! Climb on his back!"

The next thing Molly knew, the
wind was whooshing past and Super
Snuffles' ears were flapping in her
face. They were flying!

"Are you all right, young
Molly?" came a shout from behind.
She turned to see the Captain
clutching on to Super Snuffles' tail,
his legs flailing about and his cape

billowing in the wind.

"I think so, Grandad!" she
shouted back. "But this is certainly
turning out to be an extraordinary
day!"

Eventually they landed in front of a
large gate. Behind it stood a house.
It was ordinary in every sort of

way, except that it was huge and painted a striking red colour.

"There it is, Molly," said the Captain. "If Super Snuffles' nose is right, then that's where the Scarlet Sorceress lives, and where she's holding your parents prisoner."

"So let's go and find them!" Molly said.

"Steady girl," said the Captain, holding up a green finger. "That Sorceress is very crafty. We must be careful."

They crept through the gate and found themselves in a pleasantly kept garden. It had a rockery, some nice apple trees, a few neatly trimmed rose bushes and a rich green lawn speckled with daisies.

The Captain tiptoed over to the nearest tree, pressed himself against the trunk and cautiously looked one way and the other, then signalled for the others to join him. Molly started to suspect that her mum was right, and that this superhero business was a bit silly.

"Grandad, this is just a garden," she said.

"Don't be fooled," he whispered. "It may look like just a garden but it's full of wickedness. *Follow me.*"

They tiptoed from one tree to another and then on to the next, each one taking them closer to the home of the Sorceress.

"So far so good," whispered the Captain. "Now for the final dash."

But just as the three made a run
for the house, they were suddenly
whisked into the air. They were
trapped!

Wicklow County Council
County Library Services

4. Rock Cakes

Molly, Super Snuffles and the Captain swung helplessly from a tree. Molly was shaken, but the Captain remained calm. "We seem to be caught in a woollen net," he mused. "I think this must be the work of the WWI."

"That's right," came a shriek. "We knitted it ourselves!"

Molly peered out through the gaps in the net and saw six or seven elderly ladies come dancing out from behind a nearby rockery.

"Right, girls," screamed one of them. "Get the pot!" Two of the ladies skipped off and came back pushing a large saucepan on wheels. It was full of some kind of foul-smelling liquid.

"Soup!" cried the Captain. "What sort is it – carrot and coriander? Broccoli and Stilton? Cream of tomato?"

"Aaarch no!" spluttered the women. They screwed up their faces and spat on the ground. "We hate that sort of thing. This is mud and pig-spit soup, and it's delicious," they said, licking their lips, "but it needs something else, something special!"

"Don't tell me, would that 'something special' just happen to be . . . cucumber?" asked the Captain.

"YES!" squealed the ladies, clapping their hands with delight.

"What are we going to *do*?" Molly asked the Captain.

"To be honest, I haven't the foggiest idea," he said. Then he grinned. "Don't worry, something will turn up."

"*COO-EE!*" came a cry from the sky.

They all looked up. There was Great Aunt Nelly, the lollipop lady.

She was riding her lollipop stick
through the sky! "Mind fingers!"
she sang and she swooped down,
slicing through the net with the edge
of her sign.

"Hooray for Lollipop Lady!"
hollered the Captain as they sprang
free.

28

The wicked women shouted
something very rude and scattered
behind bushes and trees. When they
reappeared, they were clutching
wicker-baskets. One of them pulled
something small and brown from
her basket and threw it at Lollipop
Lady.

"Watch out!" yelled the Captain.
"It's a rock cake – they're lethal!"

Quick as a flash, Lollipop Lady leapt to one side and batted it back with her lollipop stick. It struck the wicked woman and sent her cartwheeling through the air.

Another wicked woman pulled a greyish-looking thing from her basket and sent it spinning like a frisbee towards the Captain.

"It's a UFF," cried Lollipop

Lady. "An Unidentified Flying Flan!"

In one smooth movement the Captain pulled a seed from the pouch on his belt and tossed it at the UFF. In a flash of green smoke, the flan was transformed into a prize cucumber and struck the Captain's chest with a harmless squelch.

"You can change things into cucumbers, Grandad!" gasped Molly. "No wonder you win all those gardening prizes."

Captain Cucumber paused to scowl at his granddaughter. "I may be many things, my dear, but I'm no cheat," he said. "I won those trophies fair and – *WATCH OUT!*"

Molly turned to see a wicked woman almost upon her.

"Look what I've knitted for you, little girl," she shrilled, brandishing a large jumper. "Try it on for size!"

"Don't do it!" cried Lollipop Lady. "That jumper's got no neck-hole! It's nothing more than a bag to trap you in!"

What could Molly do? She

wasn't a superhero. She had no
superpowers, and Captain
Cucumber and Lollipop Lady were
busy fending off a hail of nasty
cakes. Desperately she looked

around for a stick or something she could use to defend herself, but there was nothing. She searched her pockets, but all she had was a bag of sweets. It wasn't much of a dangerous weapon, but what choice did Molly have? Pulling out an

aniseed twirl, she threw it straight into the wicked woman's gaping mouth.

"Arrgh, a disgusting sweetie!" gagged the woman.

Then she fell flat on her back!

After a moment, she sat up and, looking rather bewildered, said, "Oh dear, I've been so terribly wicked . . . please forgive me."

"That's it!" cried the Captain. "Of course, witches hate nice things like sweeties; they destroy their wickedness. Well done, that girl!"

The other wicked women regrouped, hitched up their skirts, and ran at them in one last desperate attack. Molly pulled a sherbet fountain from her pocket,

tore out the liquorice straw and
shook the white powder high in the
air over each and every one of
them. The wicked women fell to the
ground, screeching and arching and
twisting and pulling at their hair
and clothes. Then they fell silent
and still. Finally, they sat up,

changed like their friend into the
nice ladies they had once been, and
apologized for their wickedness.

"Go home," ordered the Captain.
"Go home to your families, to your
grandchildren. Go home to your
cats and canaries. For you, the
nightmare is over."

Slowly, one by one, the ladies clambered to their feet and filed out through the front gate.

"That was the easy bit," sighed the Captain. "Now we've got to find your parents. Heaven knows what that wicked witch has done with them."

"So how can we find them?" asked Molly.

"Simple," said Lollipop Lady. "We'll find them the same way I found you, my dear – by looking in my special lollipop sign." They gazed at the sign and slowly the words "STOP. CHILDREN CROSSING" faded, and in their place appeared a table and a chair.

"Those aren't my parents,"

Molly cried. "That's furniture!"

The Captain put his hand on her
shoulder. "She's used her black
magic to turn them both into
furnishings for her house," he said.
"Molly . . . we may be too late."

"No!" cried Molly. "Nooooooo!" She ran up the garden path towards the big, red house.

"WAIT!" cried the Captain. "She's in there waiting for you, Molly. You don't understand what danger you're in!"

Deaf to the Captain's warning, Molly pulled open the enormous front door and ran inside.

5. Furniture

In front of Molly lay a huge
room. It was full of the most
elegant furniture and the most
expensive-looking ornaments she
had ever seen in all her life. Then
Molly saw someone walking slowly
down the stairs: a great gangling
woman in a scarlet jumpsuit. Her
neck glistened with jewels, and her

hair was a column of dusty blue. It was the Scarlet Sorceress herself.

"Looking for me?" she said.

The next moment, Molly's super-relatives were at her side.

"Ah, a family reunion," smiled the Sorceress. "How charming."

"We're not here for any reunion with you!" bellowed the Captain. "Super Snuffles – *get her!*"

The trusty mutt leapt forward, gnashing his teeth. With a flick of her wrist the Sorceress turned him into a footstool, and he clattered to the floor.

"Right, you horrible old bag, I've had enough of this!" hollered the Captain. He sprang into the air scattering a fistful of seeds over the

witch. With a wave of her hand she
turned all the seeds into scatter
cushions, and they tumbled down
around her, bouncing softly on to
the carpet.

"You were supposed to turn into a prize cucumber, old girl!" the Captain exclaimed.

"Not today thank you, *old boy*," she cackled, and WHAM! she turned him into a grandfather clock.

"Stop!" ordered Lollipop Lady, holding her stick high.

"Stop? I've hardly started, dear sister," the Sorceress hooted. "Be a fridge – that'll cool you down." And BLAM! poor Lollipop Lady became a big, white fridge and her stick fell flat on to the carpet.

Then the Sorceress turned her gaze to Molly. "I planned this all for you, my dear. Stealing your parents, leaving the note, it was all just a way to lure you here. I am getting old and soon I will need someone to carry on my wickedness, someone with special powers like my own, and that someone is you."

"But I haven't any special powers." Molly said.

"Oh, but yes you have," the Sorceress clucked. "Witchcraft is strong in you, I can feel it. Join me and we can be bad together!"

"Never!" Molly cried and dug
deep into her pocket where she
found one last sweetie – a toffee
royal. She pulled it out and tossed
it right between the scarlet lips of
the Sorceress. The great witch
crunched on it and swallowed.

"You'll need a bigger sweetie than that to get me," she hissed and slowly raised a bony finger. "So you refuse to join me . . . then be a floppy snake! You can spend the rest of your days at the foot of my door – keeping the draught out."

Quickly, Molly grabbed the lollipop stick and hid behind it. SHAZAM! It became a floppy snake.

"NO!" Molly heard herself shout. "Be a lollipop again, this time a *real* lollipop!"

And, to her utter astonishment, that's exactly what happened.

The Sorceress staggered backwards, her eyes wide with surprise.

"Is *this* sweetie big enough for
you?" Molly cried, and flung the
lollipop straight into the Sorceress's
gaping mouth. The witch fell flat on

her back. There was a crash of
thunder, a flash of lightning and a
great plume of smoke. When it
cleared, there stood an ordinary-
looking, elderly lady.

"Oh my," she said. "I think I've
been a bit of a bad girl."

6. Reunion

The lady was, of course, Molly's long-lost Great Aunt Gerty. With her wickedness destroyed, her house and garden turned back into the rubbish dump it once was, and all her pieces of furniture turned back into the people they once were, and that included Molly's parents, thank goodness.

Everyone forgave Great Aunt Gerty for being so naughty and there were big hugs all around, so it did turn out to be a bit of a family reunion after all.

As there were too many people to fly back on Super Snuffles, they all decided to walk home.

Every time they came to a busy

road, Great Aunt Nelly stopped the traffic so they could all cross over safely.

"Oh dear, I've just remembered," said Great Aunt Gerty as they walked up the path to Grandad's house. "I turned a lot of people into furniture and sold them to finance the WWI."

"Do you mean to say there are people up and down the country who are suddenly discovering that their sofas and chairs are, in fact, people?" exclaimed Grandad.

"Well, yes," said Great Aunt Gerty sheepishly.

Grandad roared with laughter. "You can't help but see the funny side, old girl," he cried, and soon everyone else was laughing too, even Great Aunt Gerty, although she tried hard not to.

After dinner, Molly was formally made the newest superhero in the family.

"Do you promise to use your powers for good things and not for bad?" asked Grandad.

Wicklow County Council
County Library Services

"I do," said Molly.

"And do you promise to keep your room tidy and eat all your greens?" asked her mum.

"No way!" laughed Molly. "I'm not *that* superhuman!"

Leabharlann Chill Mhantáin

3 0006 00102923 1